THE 26-STORY TREEHOUSE

ANDY GRIFFITHS

illustrated by Terry Denton

Feiwel and Friends • New York

A FEIWEL AND FRIENDS BOOK
An imprint of Macmillan Publishing Group, LLC

THE 26-STORY TREEHOUSE. Text copyright © 2012 by Backyard Stories
Pty Ltd. Illustrations copyright © 2012 by Terry Denton. All rights reserved.
Printed in the United States of America by LSC Communications,
Harrisonburg, Virginia. For information, address Feiwel and Friends,
175 Fifth Avenue, New York, N.Y. 10010.

Feiwel and Friends books may be purchased for business or promotional use
For information on bulk purchases, please contact the Macmillan Corporate
and Premium Sales Department at (800) 221-7945 x5442 or by e-mail at
specialmarkets@macmillan.com.

Library of Congress Cataloging-in-Publication Data Available
ISBN: 978-1-250-02691-0 (hardcover) / 978-1-250-06012-9 (ebook)

Feiwel and Friends logo designed by Filomena Tuosto

Originally published as *The 26-Storey Treehouse*
in Australia by Pan Macmillan Australia Pty Ltd

First published in the United States by Feiwel and Friends,
an imprint of Macmillan

First U.S. Edition: 2014

20 19 18 17 16 15 14 13 12

mackids.com

CONTENTS

CHAPTER 1

THE 26-STORY TREEHOUSE

Hi, my name is Andy.

This is my friend Terry.

We live in a tree.

Well, when I say "tree," I mean treehouse. And when I say "treehouse," I don't just mean any old treehouse—I mean a 26-*story* treehouse! (It used to be a 13-story treehouse, but we've added another 13 stories.)

So, what are you waiting for?
Come on up!

We've added a bumper car rink,

a skate ramp (with a crocodile-pit hazard),

a mud-fighting arena,

an antigravity chamber,

an ice-skating pond (with real, live ice-skating penguins),

a recording studio,

a mechanical bull called Kevin,

14

an ATM (that's an Automatic Tattoo Machine, in
case you didn't know),

an ice-cream parlor with seventy-eight flavors, run by an ice cream-serving robot called Edward Scooperhands,

and the Maze of Doom—a maze *so* complicated that nobody who has gone in has *ever* come out again.

As well as being our home, the treehouse is also where we make books together. I write the words and Terry draws the pictures.

As you can see, we've been doing this for quite a while now.

Sure, Terry can be a bit annoying at times . . .

23

but mostly, we get on pretty well.

CHAPTER 2

THE STORY OF HOW WE MET

If you're like most of our readers, you're probably wondering how Terry and I met. Well, it's a long story, but it's a pretty exciting one and it starts like this. . . .

Once upon a time
in a faraway land,
there was a very big city ...

27

and at the top of that very tall tower, there was an apartment . . .

and in that apartment, there lived a little boy who was very lonely . . .

RING! RING!

RING! RING!

RING! RING!

Excuse me for a minute. That's our video phone.
I'd better answer it. It's probably Mr. Big Nose,
our publisher.

Yep, I was right. It's Mr. Big Nose. Nobody else in the world has a nose that big.

"What took you so long?" he says. "I'm a busy man, you know!"

"But it was only six rings," I say.

"Don't argue!" he says. "I'm a busy man—I don't have time to argue. How's the new book going?"

"So far, so good," I say. "I'm telling the story of how Terry and I met."

"Great idea!" says Mr. Big Nose. "How *did* you two clowns meet, anyway?"

"Well, it's a long story," I say, "but it's a pretty exciting one, and—"

"I don't have time to listen to long stories," says

Mr. Big Nose. "Save it for the book. Just make sure it's on my desk by next Friday!"

The screen goes blank.

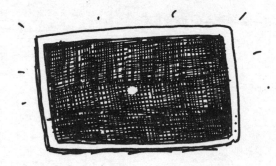

Friday?

But that's only next week!

That doesn't leave much time. I'd better get moving. Now, where was I? Let me see . . .

The faraway land . . .

the very big city . . .

the very tall tower . . .

33

"Andy!" says Terry, bursting into the kitchen. "We've got a problem!"

"What sort of problem?" I say.
"The sharks are sick!"
"What's the matter with them?"
"They ate my underpants!"

CHAPTER 3

WHY THE SHARKS ATE TERRY'S UNDERPANTS

I look at Terry for a minute as I try to understand what he just said.

"I'm sorry," I say. "I must have misheard you. It sounded like you said the sharks ate your *underpants*."

"I *did* say that!" says Terry. "And now the sharks are really sick! They're just lying on the bottom of the tank not moving."

"But *why* did they eat your underpants?" I say. "I mean, how did they even *get* them?"

"Well," he says, "I came up with the idea of using the shark tank to wash my underpants. I dangled a dummy over the top of the water and the sharks thought it was a real person, and were jumping all around trying to bite it, and that churned up the water—you know, like in a washing machine.

"So then I put my underpants on the end of a stick and lowered them into the water.

"But the sharks were jumping around so much, they knocked the underpants off the stick and then they ate them. Now the sharks are just lying on the bottom of the tank and they've turned a weird green color!"

Green

Bottom of Tank

You know, Terry has done some dumb things in the past, but this has got to be the dumbest ever!

The top 5 dumbest things Terry has ever done.

5. Put gelatin (lots) in the penguin bath.

4. Rode his horse along the beach and past the sign that read <u>DANGER</u>: <u>QUICKSAND</u>.

3. Went rowing with his elephant friend.

2. Took his boa constrictor to a movie.

EXIT

1. Tried to wash his underpants in the shark tank.

39

"What are we going to do, Andy?" says Terry.

"I'm not sure," I say. "If only we knew somebody who loves animals and knows all about them and lives close by so they could get here in a hurry."

"Yeah," says Terry, "somebody like Jill."

"Yeah," I say, "somebody *exactly* like Jill."

"Hey, I know!" says Terry. "Why don't we call Jill?"

"Great idea!" I say.

In case you don't know who Jill is, she's our neighbor. She lives just on the other side of the forest and she loves animals and knows all about them. She's got two dogs, a goat, three horses, four goldfish, one cow, six rabbits, two guinea pigs, one camel, one donkey, and thirteen flying cats.

Terry leaps up. "I'll call her on the video phone right now!"

"But Jill doesn't have a video phone," I say.

"No problem," says Terry. "I'll use my new super-flexible, endlessly extendable, titanium-coated talking tube instead."

43

45

46

47

"Hey, Jill," says Terry. "Can you come over right away?"

"I'm kind of busy right now," says Jill. "I'm having a tea party with my catnaries."

"But it's urgent!" says Terry. "The sharks are sick!"

"What's wrong with them?" says Jill.

"They ate my underpants," says Terry.

"Your *underpants*?" says Jill. "Oh no! How many pairs?"

"Three," says Terry.

"I hope they were clean," says Jill.

"Well, no," says Terry. "That's the thing, you see—I was trying to wash them."

"OH NO!" says Jill. "I'm on my way—meet you at the shark tank!"

"Here she is now!" says Terry.

"Wow," I say. "That was fast!"

"Yes," says Jill, "these flying cats are great! Turning Silky into a catnary was the best thing you ever did, Terry—unlike feeding your underpants to the sharks, which has got to be pretty much the *worst*."

Jill peers into the tank. "The poor things," she says. "I'd better get in and take a closer look."

We watch as Jill and her cats dive into the tank and get to work.

She tries aquapuncture...

dorsal-fin massage...

guided meditation...

shark aerobics . . .

and motivational movies . . .

but nothing seems to work.

Finally, Jill rises to the surface. "They're definitely the sickest sharks I've ever seen," she says. "They're so sick, in fact, that I'm going to have to operate."

"Operate?!" I say.

"Yes," says Jill. "I'm going to have to perform open-shark surgery!"

CHAPTER 4

OPEN-SHARK SURGERY

You've got to hand it to Jill. She really loves animals. Even sharks.

I mean, I *like* animals, and I think sharks are really cool, but there's NO WAY I'd ever get in a tank and operate on them, not even if they're too sick to move.

And judging by the way Terry is trembling, he's not too keen on the idea, either.

"Well," I say,
"I guess we'll leave
you to it.
Good luck!"

"Where do you think
you're going?" says Jill.
   "To the kitchen,"
I say. "I'm kind of in
the middle of telling
the readers
a story."

"Yeah," says Terry.
"I'd better go as well—
Andy will need me
to draw the pictures."

"Oh no, you don't," says Jill. "Both of you are staying right here—I need you to help me with the operation."

"But what about the readers?" I say.

"Don't worry," says Jill. "I'll deal with them."

"Excuse me, readers! Unfortunately, we've got a bit of an emergency here and I'm just going to have to borrow Andy and Terry for a moment. Is that okay? Great! Thanks for understanding. And do feel free to watch! Just try not to sneeze—we don't want any more germs getting into these poor sharks."

She turns back to us.

"I've explained the situation to the readers and they're fine with it, so get your diving suits on and let's get started."

We shrug, put on our diving suits, and follow Jill into the tank.

I don't know if you've ever been in a tank full of man-eating sharks before but, believe me, it's pretty scary. The sharks look even bigger down here than they do from up there.

"What if the sharks wake up and get hungry while we're doing the surgery?" I say.

"They won't," says Jill. "Trust me. But just to be sure, I'll give them each a dose of Dr. Numbskull's Sleepy Shark Sleeping Potion."

"Can I just ask one question?" I say.

"Sure," says Jill.

"Aren't we underwater?"

"Yes, of course we are," she says.

"Then, how come we can talk?"

"Sorry, Andy, but that's two questions and we only had time for one. Are you ready?"

"Yes, but what do we do?" says Terry. "I've never operated on a shark before."

"It's not so hard," says Jill. "You know how to work a zipper, don't you?"

"Yes."

"Well, there's one about halfway down its belly. Just unzip it and empty the contents."

"Wow!" I say. "I never knew sharks had zippers!"

I unzip my shark and peer into its belly. As you might expect, it's full of fish. I can't see any sign of Terry's underpants, but I can see some sort of large, round object. I reach in and pull it out.

"Hey, look what I found! It's Captain Woodenhead's wooden head!"

"Yikes!" says Terry.

"Ugh," says Jill. "That's really creepy."

Jill's right. It *is* really creepy.

Even though the eyes are made of wood, it feels like they are looking right at you.

And it's quite a coincidence, really, because Captain Woodenhead is actually tied up with that whole story I was telling you earlier about how Terry and I met.

You remember that lonely little boy? The one at the top of the very tall tower? Well . . .

"Andy!" says Jill. "Stop talking to the readers! Do I have to remind you that we're in the middle of open-shark surgery? Let's focus and get this job finished—then you can blather away all you want."

"I'm not 'blathering,'" I say. "I'm *narrating*."

Jill and Terry look at each other, roll their eyes, and smile.

"Whatever," says Jill. "Just save it till later."

"Hey, look what I found!" says Terry, holding up a pair of underpants.

"And I just found a pair, too," I say, pulling them out of my shark.

"And here's the third pair," says Jill, holding them as far away from herself as possible. "Terry, these underpants are disgusting!"

"I know!" he says. "That's why I was trying to wash them!"

"Will the sharks be all right now?" I say.

"I hope so," says Jill. "I think the best thing for them is to be zipped back up and have a good rest. The cats and I can take it from here."

CHAPTER 5

TERRY'S STORY

Back in the kitchen, our automatic marshmallow
machine senses how hungry we are and begins
firing marshmallows into our mouths.

"So," says Terry, through a mouthful of marshmallows, "what story were you telling the readers when I interrupted you?"

"I was telling them the story of how we met," I say.

"Oh, I love that story!" says Terry. "We were both lost in the forest . . .

and then we met and found that house made of gingerbread . . .

and we started eating it and a nice little old lady
came out and invited us in . . .

and then she put you in a cage to fatten you up
so she could eat you—which, come to think of it,
really wasn't a very nice thing for a nice little old
lady to do—

so I pushed her into the oven—which, come to think of it, wasn't a very nice thing for me to do, but—"

"Terry," I say, "that's not the story of how we met . . . that's *Hansel and Gretel*—it's a fairy tale!"

(Remember how I told you that Terry can be a bit annoying at times? Well, this is one of those times.)

Terry frowns and looks confused. "Oh, yeah . . . my mistake," he says. "I remember now. I was taking some food to my sick grandmother and I met you in the woods.

You had big eyes . . .

big teeth . . .

and you were covered in fur in those days . . .

Later, you dressed up in my grandmother's clothes
. . . I never really understood why you did that."

"I *didn't* do that!" I say. "And that's not how we met, either. That's *Little Red Riding Hood*!"

Terry smacks his head. "It is? Of course! Sorry, Andy—how could I be so dumb? Hang on, I've got it. There was a castle . . .

We met at the ball and danced . . .

But when the clock struck twelve, you went
running off and lost your glass slipper.

I looked everywhere for you. I searched the
kingdom, far and wide, but—"

"Terry!" I yell. "You're not even close! That's *Cinderella*!"

Terry shrugs. "Then I give up. I've got no idea how we met."

"Well," I say, "if you promise to be quiet for the next twenty-one pages, I'll tell you."

"Okay," says Terry. "I promise."

Once upon a time in a faraway land, there was a very big city . . .

and in that very big city, there was a very tall tower . . .

and at the top of that very tall tower, there was an apartment . . .

and in that apartment, there lived a little boy who was very lonely.

The little boy was very lonely because he didn't have any friends. And the reason he didn't have any friends was because his parents thought friends were too dangerous.

In fact, they thought *everything* was too dangerous. They never even let the little boy out of the apartment.

He lived in a padded room,

slept in a padded, non-fall-outable bed,

and sat in a padded, non-fall-outable chair, which, for extra safety, was fitted with air bags and a seatbelt.

He wasn't allowed to watch TV.

He wasn't allowed to play on the computer.

And he wasn't allowed to play with toys
or any other sort of game.

All he had to amuse himself with were books (with rounded corners) that his parents had selected for him.

These books contained no harmful ideas, no characters doing dangerous things, nor any stories involving dangerous—or potentially dangerous—situations, which meant that they didn't contain much of anything at all, really.

The lonely little boy couldn't even eat proper food. His parents mashed and pureed all his food to make sure he didn't choke, and served it cold to make sure he didn't burn himself.

That is, until one day when his parents decided that even cold, mashed-up food posed too much of a risk, so they put the little boy on an IV drip instead.

And, as if all that wasn't enough, his parents also filled the apartment with every type of safety alarm possible. They had fire alarms, flood alarms, burglar alarms, spider alarms, tiger alarms, vampire alarms, false-alarm alarms, and false-alarm-alarm alarms.

They also had the little boy fitted with a pair of emergency self-inflating underpants just in case he ever fell into water.

Now, you might think emergency self-inflating underpants are a really crazy idea, considering the little boy never even left the apartment, but you would be wrong because, as it turned out, they saved the little boy's life.

One night, while everybody was sleeping, a circuit board overloaded with too many safety devices overheated and caught on fire.

The little boy was woken by the fire alarm. He got out of bed and ran to the door, but his way was blocked by smoke and flames.

He ran to the window but, of course, it was locked.

So, the little boy picked up his safety chair, threw it at the window, and smashed a big hole in it.

And then he climbed through the broken window and stood on a ledge outside of the building.

This was by far the most dangerous situation the little boy had ever been in. Well, actually, it was the only *dangerous* situation he'd ever been in.

He looked down at the ground below—a long, long, long way below.

He looked back into his bedroom, which was now completely on fire.

He knew jumping from the top floor of a very tall apartment tower was an extremely dangerous thing to do, but he knew that staying in a burning apartment was extremely dangerous, too. Possibly even more extremely dangerous than jumping from the top floor of a very tall apartment tower.

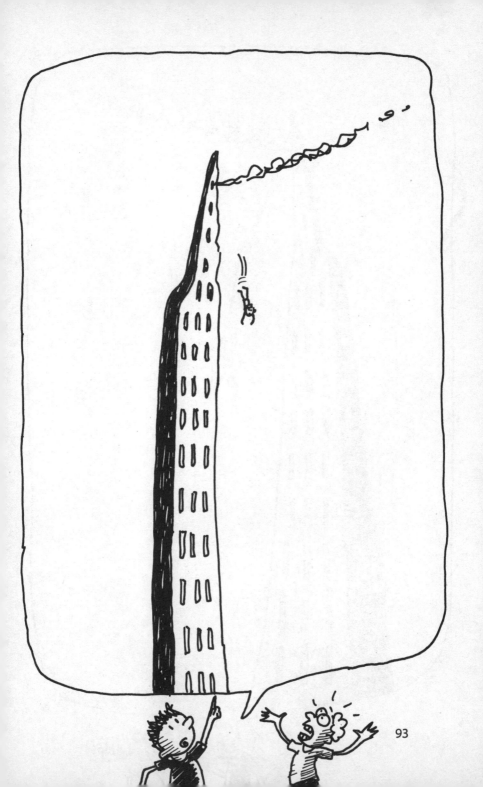

93

94

95

He hit a tree . . .

and then bounced off that tree . . .

into another tree . . .

and then bounced off that tree . . .

and hit another tree . . .

and then hit a few more trees . . .

before falling—with a big splash—into a nearby river.

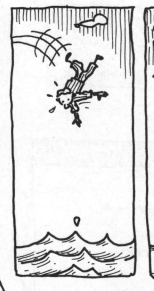

The little boy couldn't swim, but as soon as he hit the water, his emergency self-inflating underpants activated and away the little boy floated . . .

down the river . . .

and, eventually, far out to sea.

"Was he all right?" says Terry.

"Well, as a matter of fact, he was," I say. "Because I rescued you in a pedal boat."

"Me?" says Terry.

"Yes, because *you* were the boy in the story."

"I was? . . . Oh yes, now I remember . . . it *was* me!
Of course . . . it was me all along . . . but what were
you doing in a pedal boat?"

"Well, that's actually a whole other story," I say.

"Is it a long story?"

"Kind of."

"Can we get an ice cream first?"

"What a good idea!" I say. "Let's go visit Edward
Scooperhands."

THIS WAY TO THE ICE-CREAM PARLOR

CHAPTER 6

ANDY'S STORY

At the ice cream parlor, I get a double-scoop chocolate ice cream but, as usual, Terry can't decide what flavor he wants.

"Hurry up," I say, "the readers are waiting!"

"I'm sorry," he says, "but there are seventy-eight flavors here. I don't want to make the wrong decision."

"Maybe you could ask the readers to help you choose," I say.

"Great idea!" says Terry. "I'll do that."

"I'll have one with everything, thanks, Edward," says Terry.

"One-with-everything-coming-right-up," says Edward Scooperhands as his scooper hands go into super, high-speed scooping mode.

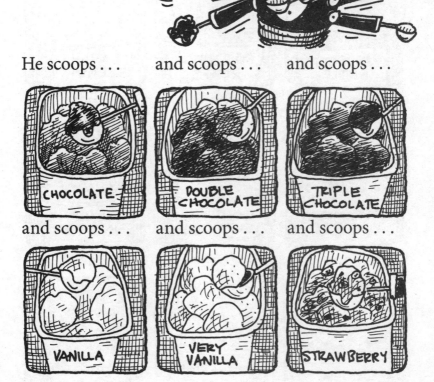

He scoops . . . and scoops . . . and scoops . . .

CHOCOLATE

DOUBLE CHOCOLATE

TRIPLE CHOCOLATE

and scoops . . . and scoops . . . and scoops . . .

VANILLA

VERY VANILLA

STRAWBERRY

and scoops . . . CHERRY

and scoops . . . STRAWBERRY AND CHERRY

and scoops . . . CHERRY AND STRAWBERRY

and scoops . . . RASPBERRY RIPPLE

and scoops . . . BLUEBERRY BURST

and scoops . . . BANANA BLAST

and scoops . . . WATERMELON WHAMMY

and scoops . . . GOLDFISH SURPRISE

and scoops . . . FLYING MONKEY

and scoops . . . EASTER EGG

and scoops . . . DEEP-FRIED DOUGHNUT

and scoops . . . PIZZA

and scoops . . .

HAMBURGER

and scoops . . .

HOT DOG

and scoops . . .

SPAGHETTI

and scoops . . .

COOKIES
AND CREAM

and scoops . . .

CHEESE AND
BISCUITS

and scoops . . .

RUM AND
RAISIN

and scoops . . .

FISH
AND CHIPS

and scoops . . .

TOMATO
SAUCE

and scoops . . .

EGG AND
BACON

and scoops . . .

EGG AND
NO BACON

and scoops . . .

BACON
AND NO EGG

and scoops . . .

NO BACON
AND NO EGG

107

and scoops . . .

POKÉMON

and scoops . . .

SUMMER
HOLIDAY

and scoops . . .

NEW
BICYCLE

and scoops . . .

CHRISTMAS
MORNING

and scoops . . .

COCONUT

and scoops . . .

FALLING
COCONUT

and scoops . . .

BUBBLEGUM

and scoops . . .

LEMONADE

and scoops . . .

CONFETTI

and scoops . . .

BUTTERSCOTCH

and scoops . . .

HOT
BUTTERED
POPCORN

and scoops . . .

MELTED
CHEESE

and scoops . . .

and scoops . . .

and scoops . . .

PEANUT BUTTER ON TOAST

BREAKFAST IN BED

MARSHMALLOW

and scoops . . .

and scoops . . .

and scoops . . .

SNAKES AND LADDERS

CACTUS (NO SPIKES)

CACTUS (WITH SPIKES)

and scoops . . .

and scoops . . .

and scoops . . .

FRESH RAIN

ELECTRICAL STORM

BRAIN-FREEZE

and scoops . . .

and scoops . . .

and scoops . . .

CAMEL HUMP

FAIRY BREAD

BATH FOAM

and scoops . . . and scoops . . . and scoops . . .

BLUE HEAVEN

BLACK FOREST

DARK SIDE OF THE MOON

and scoops . . . and scoops . . . and scoops . . .

TOTAL ECLIPSE

BIRTHDAY CAKE

MIXED CANDY

and scoops . . . and scoops . . . and scoops . . .

LOLLYPOP

TOFFEE APPLE

DAFFODIL

and scoops . . . and scoops . . . and scoops . . .

RAINBOW

SHERBERT

HONEYCOMB

and scoops . . .

CHOC-MINT

and scoops . . .

LICORICE

and scoops . . .

INVISIBLE

and scoops . . .

TUTTI-FRUTTI

and scoops . . .

SALT AND VINEGAR

and scoops . . .

GUMMY WORM

and scoops . . .

JELLY BEAN

and scoops . . .

FUDGE

and scoops . . .

ROCKY ROAD

and scoops . . .

YELLOW BRICK ROAD

and scoops . . .

WINDING ROAD

and scoops.

DIRT ROAD

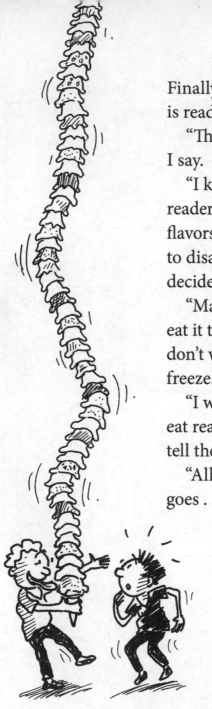

Finally, Terry's ice cream is ready.

"That's a *lot* of scoops!" I say.

"I know," he says. "But the readers all suggested different flavors and I didn't want to disappoint anyone, so I decided to have them all."

"Make sure you don't eat it too fast," I say. "You don't want to get brain-freeze."

"I won't," says Terry. "I'll eat really slowly while you tell the story."

"All right," I say, "here goes . . ."

Once upon a time there, was a little boy who had the most horrible, terrible, meanest parents in the whole wide world.

They were very strict and had all sorts of boring rules and regulations that they forced the poor little boy to follow.

For example, they made him wear shoes,

clean his teeth,

brush his hair,

wear a hat when it was sunny,

and a coat when it was cold.

They made him help out around the house,

115

do his homework,

eat with a knife and fork,

and wouldn't let him stay up all night
whenever he felt like it.

It was clear to the boy that there was never going to be an end to his parents' unreasonable rules and regulations, and he decided that he had no choice but to run away from home. And so he did.

117

The little boy loved his new life and was very happy.
Which wasn't surprising because he didn't have to
follow his parents' boring rules anymore.

He didn't have to wear shoes,

or brush his hair,

or wear a hat when it was sunny,

or a coat when it was cold,

119

and he could stay up all night whenever he felt like it, which was pretty much every night.

He found—or borrowed—all the food he needed

and became very good at building all sorts of
shelters, especially treehouses.

stupid
ice cream!!

123

One day, however, when the little boy was in a fancy restaurant borrowing some food, he accidentally knocked over one of the tables.

An angry waiter chased the boy out of the restaurant,

125

The little boy couldn't afford to hire a pedal boat, of course, so he borrowed one instead, and headed for the far side of the lake,

pedaling as fast as his little legs could pedal him.

What he didn't realize, however, was that the lake was not really a lake, but an inlet connected to the ocean, and he was carried far out to sea.

Tongue hurts...

127

He floated in his pedal boat for many days . . .

128

129

before spotting what looked like a small island with two hills in the distance.

He pedaled toward the island, but as he drew closer, he saw that it wasn't an island at all—

it was a boy, floating in an enormous pair of inflatable underpants!

"Hey," says Terry. "I've got a pair of inflatable underpants!"

"I know!" I say. "Because that boy was *you*!"

"Oh, that's right, and the boy in the pedal boat was *you*! You rescued me! And that's how we met. I love stories with a happy ending."

"But that's not the end," I say.

"It's not?"

"No, because then we were captured by Captain Woodenhead."

"Who's Captain Woodenhead?" says Terry.

"You know," I say. "Captain Woodenhead, the pirate."

"Pirate?!" says Terry. "I hate pirates!"

"Speaking of pirates," says Jill, coming into the kitchen carrying Captain Woodenhead's wooden head, "what do you want me to do with this?"

"It would make a great head for our scarecrow," says Terry.

"I didn't know you had a scarecrow," says Jill.

"We don't," says Terry, "but if we did, this head would be perfect!"

"No way," I say. "I don't want to see that man's head ever again. I hated him."

"Yeah," says Jill, "so did I."

"Oh, did you know him, too?" says Terry.

"Yes! Don't you remember? I was on board his ship when you and Andy were captured. I'll never forget my first sight of you, Terry! You looked like you were wearing a diaper!"

"It wasn't a diaper," says Terry. "I was wearing emergency self-inflating underpants. They get a bit baggy when they deflate."

"And Andy was so scared he was crying," says Jill.

"I was not crying," I say. "It was just spray from the sea."

"But how come you were on Captain Woodenhead's ship in the first place, Jill?" says Terry.

"Well, that's kind of a sad story," says Jill.

"Oh, goody," says Terry. "I *love* sad stories."

"Okay," says Jill, "but you'll have to wait until the next chapter."

"Oh," sighs Terry, disappointed.

"Don't worry," says Jill. "You won't have to wait long—it's just on the next page."

"Yay!" says Terry.

CHAPTER 7

JILL'S STORY

Once upon a time, there was a little girl who loved animals. And she didn't just love them— she could also understand them and they could understand her.

She spent every spare moment of her time with animals and helped them whenever possible.

But what the little girl wanted more than anything was a pet of her very own, and even though her parents were really rich and could have afforded to buy her millions of pets, they wouldn't let her have even one . . . not even an ant.

The only thing her parents were interested in was having parties with their fancy friends on board their luxury super yacht.

One day, the little girl was on the deck of her parents' yacht when she saw an enormous fish. It was creamy white with large, greenish-blue veins all over its body and it smelled like moldy old cheese.

The little girl, who knew everything there was to know about animals, recognized it at once as the legendary Gorgonzola—the greediest and most disgusting fish in the ocean. It stank like the stinky cheese it was named after and swam around the world eating everything in its path.

As the little girl watched in horror, Gorgonzola swam closer . . .

and closer . . .

and closer.

143

The little girl called out to her parents to warn them, but they were partying too loudly to hear her.

She leaned over the rail to ask Gorgonzola to please not eat her parents' yacht, but she leaned over too far, lost her balance, and fell into the water.

For a moment, she feared that she would become Gorgonzola's next meal, but she was so small that Gorgonzola didn't even notice her.

The little girl cried out for help but her voice could not be heard above the clink of champagne glasses and the laughter of the guests aboard the yacht.

She just bobbed helplessly in the water and watched as her parents' super yacht, pursued by Gorgonzola, vanished into the distance.

The little girl was wondering what to do next when an iceberg floated by. She climbed onto it and was astonished to find a tiny kitten sitting at the top of it.

She picked up the kitten and hugged it. She'd never felt such soft, silky fur. "I'm going to call you Silky," she said.

"Hey, that's like the name of *your* cat!" says Terry.

"That's because it *is* my cat!" says Jill. "That's how Silky and I met. This is *my* story. Remember?"

"Oh, yeah," says Terry. "I got so caught up, I forgot."

"But why was Silky floating on an iceberg in the middle of the ocean?" I say.

"Unfortunately, thousands of unwanted kittens are abandoned on icebergs every year," says Jill, tears in her eyes. "And not just kittens—it happens to lots of other animals, too. Just listen to the rest of my story and you'll see . . ."

As Silky and I floated on the iceberg,
we rescued two dogs,

a goat,

three horses,

four goldfish,

one cow,

six rabbits,

two guinea pigs,

one camel,

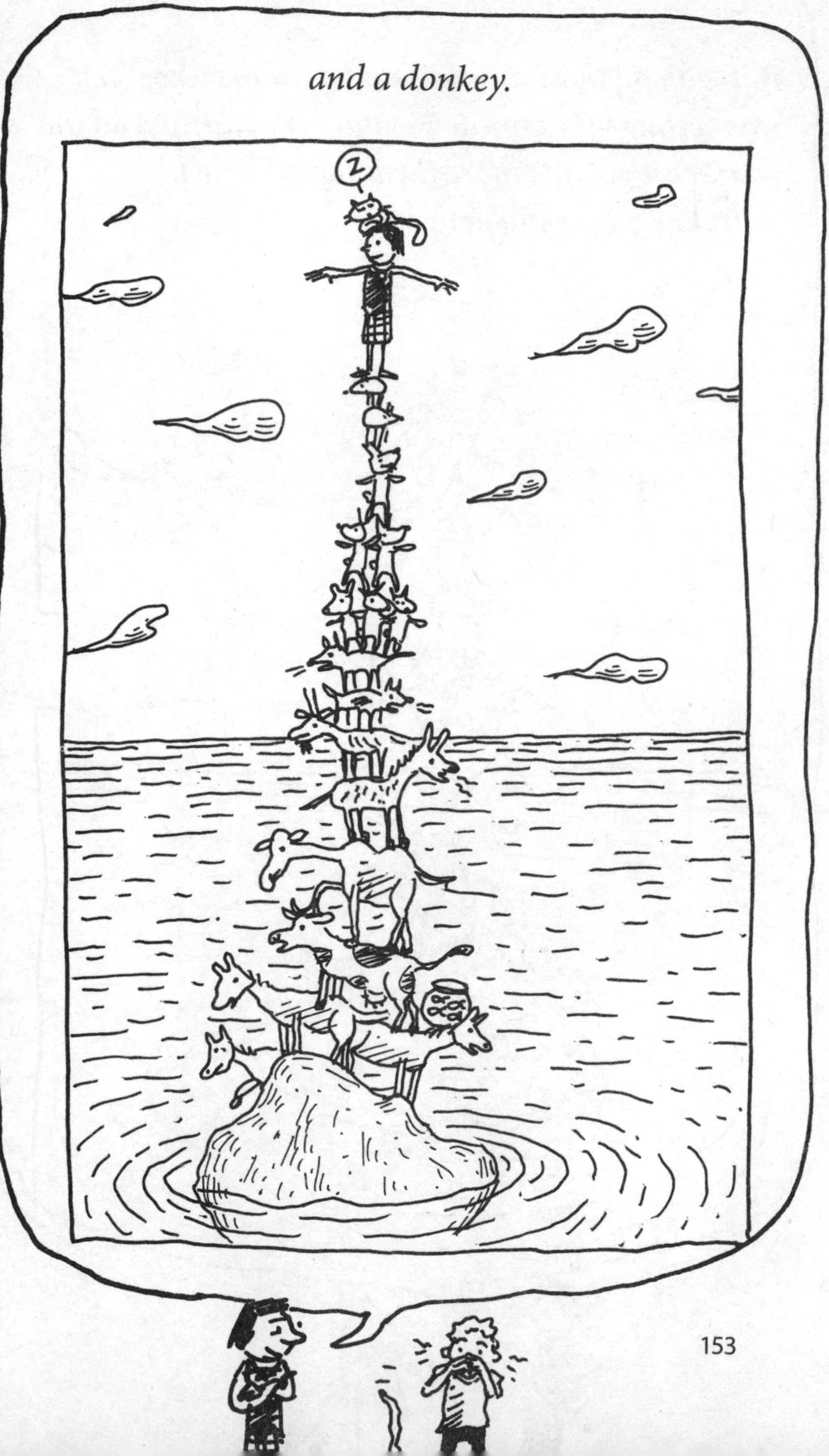
and a donkey.
Z

But with all those animals on board the iceberg, it was getting very crowded—and very warm. And the warmer it got, the more the iceberg melted.

It slowly got smaller . . .

and smaller ...

and smaller ...

155

until, finally, it was no bigger than an ice block.

"What happened then?" says Terry. "Did you all drown?"

"No, we didn't drown," says Jill. "We saw a ship."

"Thank goodness!" says Terry.

"Yeah, that's what we thought at first," says Jill. "But it turned out to be a pirate ship! And that's how I—and all the animals—came to be captured by the terrifying, horrible, and hideous pirate, Captain Woodenhead!"

"I hate pirates!" says Terry.

"Me, too," says Jill.

"And me," I say.

CHAPTER 8

WHY WE HATE PIRATES SO MUCH

Now, in case you're wondering why we hate pirates so much, it's because—as both Jill and I have already mentioned—we were all captured by a pirate. And not just *any* pirate. We were captured by the worst pirate of them all: *Captain Woodenhead.*

Do you remember that wooden head we found in the shark? If you don't, go back to page sixty-five and have a look.

THIS WAY TO PAGE 65.

If you *do* remember the wooden head, then you'll already know what a horrible-looking pirate Captain Woodenhead was and you can go straight to the start of the next paragraph and read the rest of our story—then you'll understand why we hate pirates so much.

This way to the next paragraph

As Jill has already mentioned, Captain Woodenhead was one of the most terrifying, horrible, and hideous wooden-headed pirates ever to sail the seven seas.

Sure, he rescued us all, but only to turn us into his pirate slaves . . . even the animals!

As for me and Terry and Jill, Captain Woodenhead
forced us to peel enormous piles of potatoes,

163

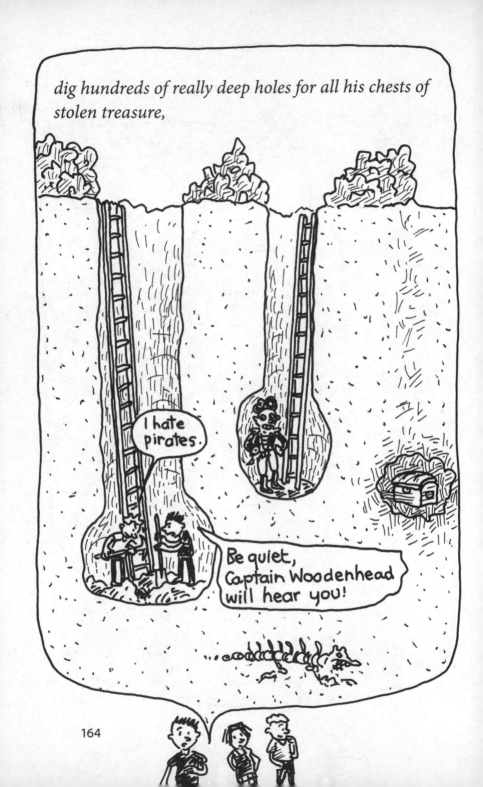

and, worst of all, he made us clean and polish the poop deck.

One day, we were cleaning the poop deck when Terry said, "I hate pirates. They're disgusting."

"How many times do I have to tell you?" I said. "Keep your voice down. Captain Woodenhead might hear you!"

"He won't hear me," said Terry. "He's only got stupid wooden ears! He's a stupid wooden-headed, wooden-eared poopy pants!"

"Hey! I heard that!" bellowed Captain Woodenhead, who was hiding behind a barrel. "I've had enough of your mutinous mutterings. It's the plank for you lot! And your stinking animals."

"No, not the animals!" said Jill. "They didn't do anything!"

"Yes they did," said Captain Woodenhead. "They're stinking up my ship, just like you and your diaper-wearing, crybaby friends. Get walking!" He pulled out his cutlass and began using it to prod us toward the plank.

"Hey, cut it out," I said, batting his cutlass away with the handle of my mop. "That thing hurts."

"Ah, so it's a fight you want, is it?" said Captain Woodenhead. "Well, I'll give you a fight. En garde!"

I barely had time to get my mop into position before he came rushing at me, waving his cutlass.

He swiped. I ducked.

I swiped. He ducked.

He swiped. I ducked.

I swiped. He ducked.

He swiped. I ducked.

BONK!

I swiped. He ducked . . .
but a little too late. BONK!

His wooden head went flying off his neck,

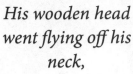

over the side of the ship,

and splashed into the water below.

169

It bobbed around on the surface for a moment before one of the sharks that were always hanging around the boat leapt out of the water and swallowed it in one gulp.

"Uh-oh," said Terry. "I don't think Captain Woodenhead's head is going to like that."

"Or his body either," said Jill. "Look out!"

Captain Woodenhead's headless body was staggering angrily around the deck, wildly swiping the heads off any crew members unfortunate enough to get in his way.

We had to get out of there—and fast—but the only safe place was the plank.

We ran out onto it—me, Terry, Jill, and all the animals.

We huddled in a big trembling bunch, hoping we'd be safe. And we were . . . but not for long. Soon, Captain Woodenhead's body came stumbling out after us.

We looked at the man-eating sharks below . . .

We looked at the angry, headless pirate with the enormous sword coming toward us . . .

We looked at each other.
"Jump?" I said.
"Jump!" said the others.
We jumped.

The sharks formed a hungry circle around us.

"Yikes!" said Terry. "We're going to be eaten alive!"

"No, we're not," said Jill. "I'll have a talk with them."

And she did. And not only did she convince them not to eat us, but she also got them to help us escape in our pedal boat, which was tied to the back of the pirate ship.

The sharks quickly chewed through the thick ropes . . .

177

and then pulled us through the water faster than any pedal boat had ever traveled before.

But as fast as we were travelling, we couldn't shake Captain Woodenhead. He was speeding after us in his ship, now wearing a lampshade in place of his head.

And just when you might have thought things couldn't get any worse, well, they did.

A huge storm blew up and it began to rain . . .

and rain . . .

and rain.

There was booming thunder . . .

bolts of lightning . . .

hailstones as big as baseballs . . .

and enormous waves.

Our little pedal boat was tossed about like a toy on the rough seas and before we knew it, we were surfing down the face of the biggest wave any of us had ever seen.

The trouble was, so was the pirate ship.

It was surfing down the wave right behind us.

That's when we saw land up ahead—well, when I say "land," I mean a wall of steep rocky cliffs.

Our little pedal boat crashed onto the rocks but, amazingly, we all managed to make it safely to shore.

The pirate ship, however, wasn't so lucky. It was smashed to pieces and we never saw Captain Woodenhead or any of his crew ever again.

Over the next few days, we collected pieces of Captain Woodenhead's broken-up pirate ship and used these to build the first level of our treehouse.

We also decided to keep the sharks because even though they're scary, they are also—as I mentioned earlier—really cool.

Meanwhile, Jill found an abandoned cottage on the other side of the forest and decided it would make a perfect home for her and all her animals.

Anyway, that's the story of how we all met and how we came to be living here and why we hate pirates so much.

"Wow," says Terry. "You're so good at telling stories, Andy. As you were describing the storm, I could practically *feel* the wind and the rain, *see* the lightning, and *hear* the thunder!"

"Yeah, me too," I say.

"Guys," says Jill, "I hate to tell you this, but the reason you can feel wind and rain, see lightning, and hear thunder is not because Andy is such a good storyteller, but because there really *is* wind and rain and lightning and thunder. There's a very big storm headed our way!"

Uh-oh. Jill's right. Looks like we're in for a rough night. We'd better stop doing the book for a while and make sure the treehouse is okay. Stay dry, and see you when the storm's over.

194

195

CHAPTER 9

FLOTSAM, JETSAM ... AND CASTAWAYS

Oh—there you are. Hello! What a night—that was some storm, huh? Hope you didn't get *too* wet.

We got a *lot* wet, and there's quite a bit of damage to the treehouse, which is why we've come down to the beach this morning to scavenge a few bits and pieces to help us fix it up again.

And there are a *lot* of bits and pieces down here because a ship was wrecked during the night.

It's quite a coincidence, actually, considering that I had just been telling you the story of how we— and Captain Woodenhead and his crew—were shipwrecked here, but I guess it's not *so* surprising because it is a *very* dangerous coastline and that was a *very* rough storm.

Everything we need is here. There are planks of wood, torn pieces of sail, barrels, wooden chests, heaps of rope, piles of potatoes . . . and even a cannon!

"Cool!" says Terry. "I've always wanted a cannon!"

"Why?" says Jill.

"Because they're really useful."

"Really useful for *what*?"

"I don't know . . . lots of stuff," says Terry. "Say if you needed to deliver something in a hurry, like . . . say . . . a book to your publisher, you could put it in the cannon and fire it over."

"Oh yeah, I didn't think of that," says Jill.

Terry and I collect armfuls of wood and rope and load them into Jill's flying-cat sleigh.

"Hey, you guys," calls Jill from farther up the beach. "Come here, quick!"

Terry and I run to join her. She's standing in front of a body lying facedown on the sand.

"He must be one of the sailors from the ship," she says.

"Look, here's another one," says Terry.

"And here's another one," I say, rushing down to the water to pull a waterlogged body onto the sand.

And then we find another . . .

and another . . .

and another . . .

and another . . .

and another . . .

and another . . .

and yet another . . .

until we've found ten in all.

"Do you think they're dead?" says Terry, poking one with a stick.

"Ouch!" says the body.

"No, I don't think so," I say. "At least not that one."

The body rolls over, sits up, and blinks.

We all gasp. And not just because we're surprised he's alive, but because of his appearance. He's *horrible*.

Although the ship was only wrecked last night, this sailor looks like he's been in the water for months. He's got mold all over his face and there are barnacles attached to his chin. And he doesn't smell too good, either—he stinks of a weird combination of rotten fish and moldy old cheese.

"Who are *you*?" he says, staring at us strangely.

"I'm Andy," I say, "and this is Terry and that's Jill. Who are you?"

"I'm the captain of the ship that was wrecked in the storm last night."

"Don't worry, we'll look after you," says Jill. "I'll get my flying cats to airlift you and your crew back to the treehouse."

"I'm sorry," says the captain. "I must be delirious . . . I thought you said *flying cats*."

"I did," says Jill. "This is Silky and her twelve flying cat friends."

"Silky?" says the captain. "I once knew a cat called Silky. But she was just a kitten. She couldn't fly, of course. Made a great slave, though."

"Slave?" says Jill, sounding shocked.

"Did I say 'slave'?" says the captain. "I meant . . . *sailor*. Like I said, I must be delirious."

"I don't want to be rude," says Terry, "but what happened to your head?"

"It's a long story," says the captain, "and not a particularly pretty one."

"Oh goody," says Terry. "I love long stories . . . especially not particularly pretty ones."

"Well, all right," says the captain. "I'll tell you if you want, but don't say you weren't warned."

CHAPTER 10

THE PIRATE CAPTAIN'S STORY

Once upon a time, there was a bad little boy who dreamed of nothing else but going to sea and becoming a pirate, and when he grew up, he did exactly that. He became a pirate captain sailing the seven seas in his very own pirate ship with his very own pirate crew.

The pirate captain spent his days plundering ships,

burying treasure,

making prisoners walk the plank,

and was as happy as any pirate captain could possibly be.

That is, until one day, when his ship was attacked by a huge disgusting fish that looked and smelled like a moldy old piece of cheese . . . a really stinky, moldy old piece of blue-green cheese.

"Gorgonzola!" says Jill.

"That's right," says the captain. "*Exactly* like gorgonzola."

"No, I mean its *name* was Gorgonzola!" says Jill.

"The very one!" says the captain. "But how would a landlubber like you know about a thing like that?"

"Jill knows everything there is to know about animals," says Terry.

"Is that right?" says the captain, studying Jill carefully before going on with his story.

The pirate captain drew his cutlass and tried to spear Gorgonzola from the deck of his ship, but as he leaned over the side, the fiendish Gorgonzola leapt right out of the water and bit the pirate's head clean off his neck!

But that pirate was a tough old sea dog and he wasn't going to let the loss of a head stop him. He carved a replacement head out of wood and from that time on, he was known as Captain Woodenhead.

"*We* knew a Captain Woodenhead!" says Terry.

"Did you now?" says the captain, turning his gaze on Terry.

"Yes," says Terry. "But he wasn't very nice. He captured us and then turned us into slaves."

"Well, shiver me timbers, that must have been the very captain I'm talking about! Were you boys in a pedal boat by any chance?"

"Yes!" I say. "A swan-shaped one!"

He turns to Jill. "And don't tell me—you were floating on an iceberg with a bunch of animals?"

"*Yes!*" says Jill. "Two dogs, a goat, three horses, four goldfish, one cow, six rabbits, two guinea pigs, one camel, one donkey, and a kitten!"

The captain looks at us, amazed. "Well, blast my non-wooden eyes!" he says. "It really *is* you! The story goes that you knocked the captain's head off with a mop!"

"Well . . . yes," I say, "but he was trying to slice *mine* off with a sword. We escaped and he chased us, but then we all got caught in a terrible storm. Our pedal boat and the pirate ship were smashed to pieces on the rocks. We were the only survivors. We used the wreckage of the pirate ship to build our treehouse. Look, you can see it up there!"

"A *pirate* ship?" the captain says slowly. "You used a PIRATE ship to build yourselves a cubbyhouse?"

"Not a cubbyhouse," says Terry, "a *treehouse*. A *thirteen-story* treehouse."

"Twenty-six, actually," I say. "We recently added thirteen more stories."

"But you had no right," says the captain. "That ship didn't belong to you."

"No, but it was wrecked and the captain and all his crew were dead," says Terry.

"That's where you're wrong," he says. "You didn't let me finish the pirate captain's story."

"Sorry," says Terry. "What happened next?"

"Well, if you'll just be quiet for the next fourteen pages, I'll tell you . . ."

After the shipwreck, Captain Woodenhead's crew were drowned, but he survived. Luckily, the lampshade he was using as a temporary head kept him afloat for many days . . . well, until he once again encountered his nemesis—Gorgonzola!

This time, though, instead of just taking his head, Gorgonzola swallowed him whole!

Oh, that fish's belly was a foul and friendless prison
in which to be trapped. They say that beast ate
everything in its path and, judging by the contents of
its disgusting stomach, it was all too true. It was like
a sea-going garbage dump in there!

Fishing rods, seagulls, shipping containers, wet suits, surfboards, Jet Skis, luxury super yachts, old World War II sea mines, barrels of dynamite, experimental armored miniature bicycle-powered submarines ... you name it, it was there. But among all the flotsam and jetsam in that stinking stomach, the captain found one thing of such incredible value that he wept when he saw it ...

It was Captain Woodenhead's original flesh-and-blood head! Sure, a little waterlogged and moldy—I'll grant you that—but otherwise, as handsome and striking a head as ever sat atop the neck of a pirate.

So then he did what any self-respecting pirate captain would have done. He collected up all the barrels of dynamite,

tied them together,

lit the fuse,

and blasted that beast to pieces!

229

230

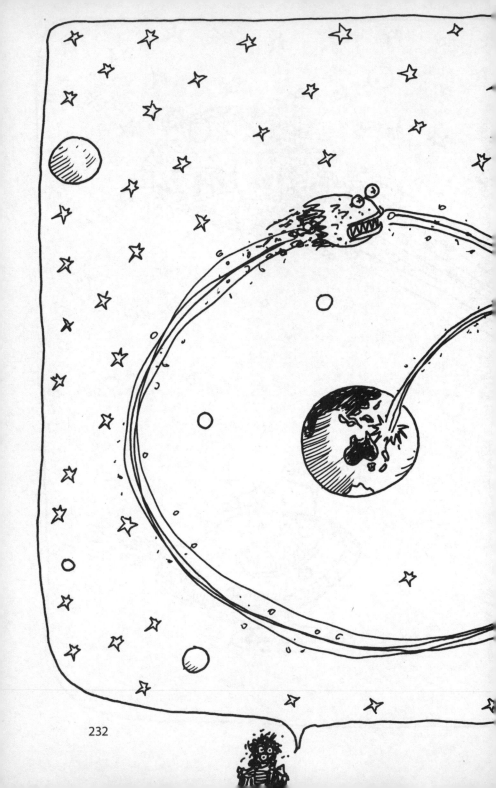

You might think that Captain Woodenhead would have been blasted to pieces, too, but he wasn't.

Safe inside the heavily armored, bicycle-powered mini submarine, he survived the explosion and made his escape.

It wasn't long before he found a suitable ship to steal,

assembled a new crew of cutthroats eager to do his bidding,

and returned to his life as a pirate.

He was as happy as could be until one night, he was caught in another terrible storm and his boat was wrecked on the very same shore that my original ship was wrecked on.

"Excuse me," says Jill, "did you say *my* original ship? Are you Captain Woodenhead?"

"Aye," says the captain. "You're a smart girl. Captain Woodenhead and myself are indeed one and the same."

"RUN!" yells Jill. "It's Captain Woodenhead!"

"Where?" says Terry, looking around.

"There!" I say, pointing at the pirate captain.

"Him?" says Terry. "But he doesn't have a wooden head."

"Weren't you listening, Terry?" says Jill. "He just told us the whole story. He found his original head in Gorgonzola's belly!"

"Yikes!" says Terry. "Let's get out of here!"

"Not so fast," says Captain Woodenhead, jumping up and grabbing us in a pirate hug (which is just like a bear hug, only pirate style). "Now I've got you, and I'm going to make you pay for what you did to me!"

"But it was all your fault!" I say. "You started it by kidnapping us and making us into slaves!"

"That may be so, but *you* knocked my head off with a mop and shipwrecked my boat and stole the pieces! So now, I'm going to claim *your* treehouse—and all who sail in it—in the name of Captain Woodenhead!"

He turns to the other castaways. "All right, you scurvy mongrels, get up! The treehouse is ours!"

At the captain's command, his crew stagger to their feet. The captain hands us over to three of the biggest ones while the others obediently begin climbing up the cliffs toward the treehouse.

We kick and struggle against our captors but it's no use. They are too strong.

"Well, I guess that's it," I say. "No more treehouse."

"Never fear," says Terry, lifting his T-shirt. "My emergency self-inflating underpants are here! Watch this!" He pulls at a small cord hanging down the front of his trousers.

Terry's underpants inflate so quickly and with such force that the pirates holding us are thrown backward onto the sand.

The three pirates jump back up, cutlasses in hand.

"Hold on to me," says Terry as he steps toward them.

"What are you doing, Terry?" says Jill. "You're wearing inflatable underpants and they've got really sharp swords!"

"I know," says Terry. "That's the idea!"

Before I can ask him what the idea is, there is a loud

followed by an enormous whoosh of air and we are blasted up into the sky.

WHOOSH!

We soar.

We dive.

We climb.

We plummet.

We loop once . . .

twice . . .

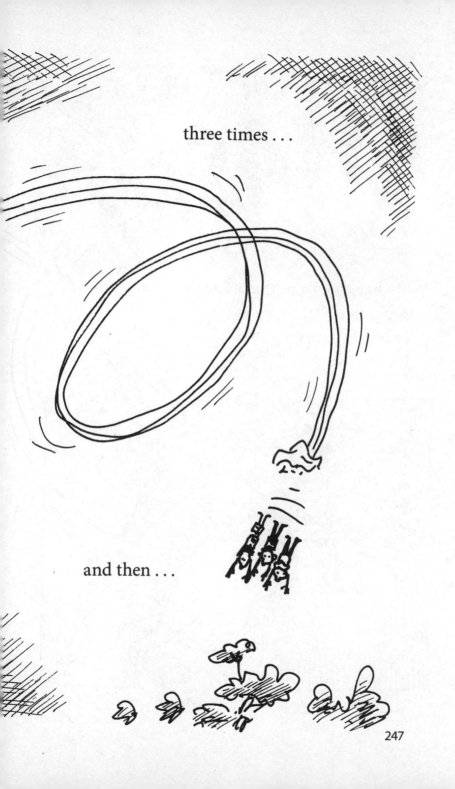

three times . . .

and then . . .

We're hanging from the branch of a tree.

A big tree.

I don't believe it.

It's *our* tree!

"Sorry about the rough ride," says Terry. "I don't really know how to fly these things."

"That's quite okay," I say, untangling myself from the tattered shards of rubber. "But what I want to know is why were you even *wearing* your emergency self-inflating underpants?"

"Because all my normal underpants are dirty," says Terry. "That's why I was washing them, remember?"

"Oh, yeah," I say. "That seems like so long ago now."

"It's only been two hundred pages," says Terry.

"Two hundred and *thirteen*, actually," says Jill. "But there won't be many more pages in this book if we don't protect the treehouse against the pirates. Look! They're already here!"

We look down. Jill's right. The pirates have already scaled the cliffs and surrounded the trunk of our tree.

CHAPTER 11

TEN UNLUCKY PIRATES

"Open up!" yells Captain Woodenhead, pounding on the door.

"Sorry," I say. "Members only!"

"Now, come on, Andy," says Captain Woodenhead.
"Let me and my crew in. I promise nothing bad
will happen. Forgive and forget, that's my motto."

"But what about that stuff you said on the beach
about 'making us pay' and how you were going to
claim our treehouse for yourself?"

Captain Woodenhead roars with laughter. "Oh, don't take any notice of that!" he says. "That was just silly pirate talk! All we want is to come in, take off our boots, rest our weary, waterlogged bones for a couple of days, and then we'll be on our way."

"Sorry," I say, "but I'm afraid the answer is still *no*."

"All right, then you leave me no option—
we're going to blast our way in!" says Captain
Woodenhead, suddenly turning nasty again. "Men,
prepare the cannon!"

"Oh no!" says Terry. "What are we going to do?"

"Let them in," I say.

"Are you crazy?" says Jill. "You're just going to *let
them in*?"

"Yes," I say. "I know it sounds crazy, but I just had an idea. Do you remember that nursery rhyme where all the pirates get killed one at a time?"

"Of course!" says Jill. "*Ten Unlucky Pirates* is one of my favorites. But how is a nursery rhyme going to help us now, even if it *does* have ten pirates in it?"

"Well," I say, "even the craziest nursery rhymes have a grain of truth in them. Take *Hey Diddle Diddle* for instance. Everybody thinks it's just a made-up story about a cow jumping over the moon, but in 1864 in Dorset, England, a cow really *did* jump over the moon."

"Really?" says Terry.

"Yes!" I say. "And in *Rock-a-Bye Baby,* there is a baby in a cradle in the treetops and when the wind blows, the cradle falls down. Well, scientific studies show that if you put a baby in a cradle in the treetops and the wind blows, the cradle—and baby—really *will* fall down."

"That's incredible!" says Terry. "Who would ever have thought that?"

"And, of course, you know *Little Miss Muffet*—"

"That actually happened to *me*!" says Jill. "I was sitting there on my tuffet eating my breakfast when along came a spider that sat down beside me and frightened me away!"

"But I thought you loved *all* animals," says Terry.

"Not spiders," says Jill. "*Nobody* likes spiders. Not even spiders like spiders."

"Well, anyway," I say, "the point is, if I'm right, then *Ten Unlucky Pirates* suggests that ten pirates and our treehouse are going to be a bad combination."

"I hope you know what you're doing, Andy," says Terry.

"Me, too," I say.

"I'll give you one last chance to surrender peacefully," bellows Captain Woodenhead. "Otherwise, I'll blast you and your treehouse to pieces in a very non-peaceful way!"

"That won't be necessary," I say. "We've had a quick meeting and decided to allow you and your crew free membership with access to all treehouse facilities, including unlimited use of the marshmallow machine, the lemonade fountain, and the ice-cream parlor."

"Well, *that's* more like it!" says the captain amid rousing cheers from his crew.

I climb down, open the door, and the pirates barge in excitedly. Within moments, they've climbed the ladder and made it up to the main level.

"Well, I must say," says Captain Woodenhead, looking around the treehouse, "you've made yourselves quite a palace out of the pieces of my boat. I think my crew and I are going to be very happy here. Very happy indeed. Especially with you three as our slaves!"

"Slaves?" says Terry. "But I thought you said if we let you in, nothing bad would happen to us."

"There are plenty of things worse than being a pirate slave, my lad," says Captain Woodenhead. "There's having your head bitten off by a huge fish that stinks like moldy old cheese—that's pretty bad. And then there's being *swallowed* by a huge fish that stinks like moldy old cheese—that's not particularly pleasant, either. Also, having your ship wrecked in a storm and the pieces stolen by thieves isn't much fun either, in case you were wondering. . . ."

WORSE THINGS THAN BEING
A PIRATE.

1. Getting cut in half so you're only ½ a pirate.
2. Being 2 pirates.
3. Being a crash-test dummy.
4. Being an automatic door that opens and shuts by itself.
5. Being Andy.
6 Being a block of Wood.
7. Andy
8. Jill
9. Silky.

"Hey, Captain!" yells one of the pirates. "Look at this vine! Come and have a swing with us!"

Captain Woodenhead's crew are standing at the edge of the deck, clinging to a vine.

"I swear by my ex-wooden head, that *is* a mighty fine vine!" says the captain. Then he turns back to us. "You three stay here. I'm just going to have a quick swing and then I'll be back to tell you how things are going to be around here from now on."

The captain runs across and, with a mighty leap, joins his crew on the vine. They push off and go swinging out wide from the treehouse.

"Well, so far so good," I say.

"What are you talking about?" says Terry. "The pirates have taken over the treehouse and we're back to being pirate slaves again!"

"Yes, but not for long," I say. "The first verse of *Ten Unlucky Pirates* is:

Ten unlucky pirates
swinging on a vine . . .
One fell off
and then there were nine.

And look what's happening: Ten pirates swinging on a vine! See what I mean about nursery rhymes containing the truth? All we have to do is wait."

"I have to admit, it *does* look pretty dangerous," says Terry. "There are ten pirates on what is clearly only a nine-pirate vine."

"Well, it can't be that dangerous," says Jill, as we watch them swing up toward the ice-skating pond. "Nobody's fallen off yet."

"No, not *yet*," I say, crossing the fingers on both of my hands, "but any moment now . . ."

There's a bloodcurdling scream as one of the pirates loses his grip and goes plummeting downward.

We peer over the edge at the pirate-shaped hole in the ground below.

"You were right!" says Terry. "But what about the others?"

"Well, they're at the ice-skating pond," I say, "which is exactly where the rhyme predicts they would be."

Nine unlucky pirates
learning how to skate . . .

"If my calculations are correct, any moment now, we should be hearing a loud crack . . ."

"Like that?" says Terry.

"*Exactly* like that," I say. "I think we can safely let the rhyme take it from here."

Nine unlucky pirates
learning how to skate . . .
One cracked through the ice
and then there were eight.

Eight unlucky pirates
riding the mechanical bull Kevin . . .

One got bucked off
and then there were seven.

THUMP!

Seven unlucky pirates
making a rockin' pirate mix . . .

One got electrocuted
and then there were six.

Six unlucky pirates
doing a synchronized dive . . .

One missed the swimming pool
and then there were five.

Five unlucky pirates
eating ice cream galore . . .

One got brain-freeze
and then there were four.

Four unlucky pirates
playing in a tree . . .

One sat in the catapult
and then there were three.

Three unlucky pirates
each getting a tattoo . . .

The ATM* malfunctioned and then there were two.

* That's an Automatic Tattoo Machine, in case you've forgotten.

Two unlucky pirates
mud-fighting in the sun . . .

One got baked hard
and then there was one.

"That's amazing, Andy!" says Terry. "Everything happened *just* like it does in the rhyme—there's only one pirate left!"

"Yes," says Jill, "but unfortunately, it's the worst one—Captain Woodenhead! And here he comes!"

"Don't panic," I say, "there's still one more verse."

One unlucky pirate
with a cutlass and a gun.
He got lost in the Maze of Doom
and then there were none.

"Well, it's kind of right," says Terry. "He's got a cutlass *and* a gun, but he's not lost in the Maze of Doom. He's not even *in* the Maze of Doom!"

"No, not yet," I say, "but he soon will be. Let's go!"

"Where?" says Terry.

"Into the Maze of Doom!"

"But it's dangerous," says Terry. "Look at the signs."

"I know what the signs say, but Captain Woodenhead is even more dangerous! He's got a cutlass *and* a gun, remember?"

"Oh yeah, good point," says Terry. "Let's go!"

CHAPTER 12

THE MAZE OF DOOM

We run into the maze.

Captain Woodenhead runs after us. Exactly as I'd hoped he would.

We turn left.

We turn right.

We turn left again.

Then right . . .

left ...

left ...

right ...

left ...

right . . .

right . . .

left . . .

right . . .

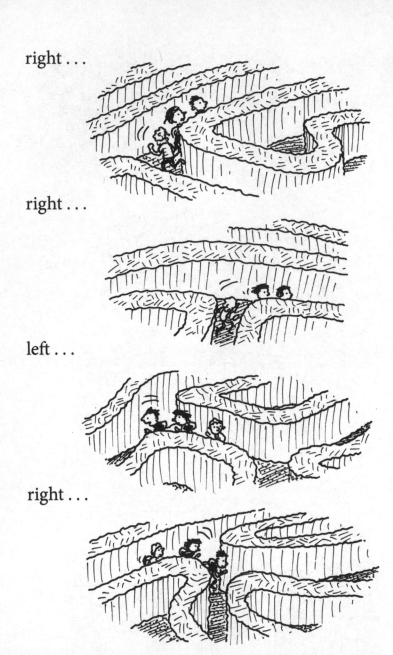

right . . .

and left . . .

until we hit a dead end.

We're all bent over double, panting.

"I think we lost him," I say.

"Yes, but now we're lost, too!" says Jill.

"No we're not," I say. "All we have to do is what we just did, but in reverse."

"But I'm not that good at running backward," says Terry.

"I don't mean that," I say. "It's a simple matter of retracing our steps. Just follow me."

We turn right . . .

then left . . .

left . . .

then right . . .

left . . .

left . . .

right . . .

left . . .

right . . .

right . . .

left . . .

right . . .

left . . .

"Unless I'm very much mistaken," I say, "we should see the entrance around the next right."

But we don't.

All we see is another dead end. And I do mean *dead*—there is a skeleton wearing a mailman's cap slumped against the wall.

"Isn't that Bill the mailman's hat?" says Jill.

"So *that's* why we haven't been getting any mail!" says Terry.

"That's so sad!" says Jill.

"I know," says Terry, "because I really *like* getting mail."

"No, I mean about Bill. I was quite fond of him."

"So was I," I say, "but it's not our fault. The warning signs are clearly posted. It's not called the Maze of Doom for nothing, you know."

"But *we* entered," says Jill.

"That's because it was an *emergency*."

"So how do we get out?" says Jill.

"We don't know," says Terry.

"What do you mean *you don't know*? You built it, didn't you? Where are the emergency exits?"

"There aren't any," I say.

"But *all* mazes have emergency exits," says Jill.

"This is the Maze of *Doom*," I explain. "It doesn't have emergency exits. That would be cheating!"

"Oh, no!" says Terry. "We're going to end up as skeletons . . . just like Bill the mailman!"

"Not necessarily," says Jill, looking skyward. "Listen."

"To what?" says Terry.

"That soft fluttering sound," says Jill. "Unless *I'm* very much mistaken, that's the sound of Silky and her friends!"

"Silky's going to save us!" says Jill. "All we have to do is follow her."

And, sure enough, Jill's right. Before long, we are making our way out of the maze . . .

and back into the safety of the treehouse.

"Thanks, Silky," says Terry. "You're an even better guide than Superfinger."

"That's because Silky is real," says Jill. "Superfinger is just a character you and Andy made up for your last book, remember?"

"Oh, yeah," says Terry.

"Speaking of books," I say, "let's get back to finishing *this* one. I don't think Captain Woodenhead will be giving us any more trouble. He'll *never* make it out of there alive."

"I wouldn't be so sure of that," says Terry, pointing behind me.

I turn to see Captain Woodenhead emerging from the maze. "But how could you possibly find your way out of there?" I gasp, as we retreat across the deck. "That's the most complicated maze in the world! It's the Maze of *Doom*!"

"A couple of lucky guesses, I suppose," says Captain Woodenhead, advancing toward us, slicing and dicing the air with his cutlass. "Well . . . lucky for me, that is—not so lucky for you."

He's right about that.

This time, there's no escape.

We're right at the edge of the deck.

Below us is the shark tank.

"You've ruined everything!" says Captain Woodenhead. "My wooden head, two of my ships, and now, you've destroyed my crew as well! But I'll have my revenge. Prepare to die!"

Captain Woodenhead raises his arm high into the air, his cutlass flashing in the sun.

"Get ready to jump," I say.

"Don't even think about it," says Jill. "Those sharks are not to be disturbed."

"Quiet, you two," says Terry, looking up. "*Listen.*"

"To what?" says Jill.

"That weird noise. Unless *I'm* very much mistaken, that's the sound of a fish head that has been blasted off its body, has gone into orbit, and is now falling back down to Earth!"

We hear a whooshing sound and look up to see the terrifying head of Gorgonzola rushing straight toward us.

Terry grabs me and Jill and pulls us clear.

Gorgonzola's head lands right on top of Captain Woodenhead!

He staggers around . . .

loses his footing . . .

and falls off the deck . . .

right into the shark tank.

There's a wild frenzy of flashing fins and teeth, and then all is quiet.

"Looks like the sharks are feeling better," says Terry.

"Yes," I say. "They've definitely got their appetite back."

"I just hope his underpants were clean," says Jill.

CHAPTER 13

THE LAST CHAPTER

You know, there's nothing like a session in the antigravity chamber to really help you relax after a stressful couple of days like the ones we've just been through.

It's so peaceful . . .
and floaty . . .
and antigravitational . . .

RING!
RING!

RING!
RING!

RING!
RING!

317

"Uh-oh," says Terry. "That's the video phone. It must be Mr. Big Nose!"

He's right. I'd better go answer it.

"What took you so long?" says Mr. Big Nose. "I'm a busy man, you know!"

"Sorry," I say. "I was relaxing in the antigravity chamber."

"Relaxing? What about the new book?"

"It's all done," I say.

"Then why isn't it on my desk?"

"Don't worry," I say, "I'll get it to you very soon, but it's been a bit hectic around here. You see—"

"Spare me the details," says Mr. Big Nose. "I don't pay you for excuses, I pay you for books, and if the new one isn't on my desk in the next five minutes, then I won't be paying you at all and you can find yourself a new publisher!"

"But I thought we had until next Friday," I say.

"You did, but the schedule changed," says Mr. Big Nose. "Five minutes . . . or else."

The screen goes blank.

"What's the matter, Andy?" says Jill.

"It's the new book," I say. "The schedule has been changed. Instead of being due next week, now it's due in five minutes."

"I hate Mr. Big Nose," says Terry.

"Be quiet," I say. "He might hear you!"

"What new book are you talking about?" says Jill.

"This one!" I say. "It's about how me and Terry met. You're in it as well."

"Really?" says Jill. "Can I see it?"

"Sure."

Once upon a time in a faraway land, there was a very big city . . .

and in that very big city, there was a very tall tower . . .

26

27

"Here she is now!" says Terry.

"Wow," I say. "That was fast!"

"Yes," says Jill, "these flying cats are great! Turning Silky into a catnary was the best thing you ever did, Terry—unlike feeding your underpants to the sharks, which has got to be pretty much the *worst.*"

Jill peers into the tank. "The poor things," she says. "I'd better get in and take a closer look."

We watch as Jill and her cats dive into the tank and get to work.

50

51

I don't know if you've ever been in a tank full of
man-eating sharks before but, believe me, it's pretty
scary. The sharks look even bigger down here than
they do from up there.

"What if the sharks wake up and get hungry while
we're doing the surgery?" I say.
"They won't," says Jill. "Trust me. But just to be
sure, I'll give them each a dose of Dr. Numbskull's
Sleepy Shark Sleeping Potion."

For example, they made him wear shoes,

clean his teeth,

Good boy.

← mirror

brush his hair,

wear a hat when it was sunny,

and a coat when it was cold.

They made him help out around the house,

114

115

until, finally, it was no bigger than an ice block.

156

"What happened then?" says Terry. "Did you all drown?"

"No, we didn't drown," says Jill. "We saw a ship."

157

323

The trouble was, so was the pirate ship.

It was surfing down the wave right behind us.

We all gasp. And not just because we're surprised he's alive, but because of his appearance. He's *horrible*.

Although the ship was only wrecked last night, this sailor looks like he's been in the water for months. He's got mold all over his face and there are barnacles attached to his chin. And he doesn't smell too good, either—he stinks of a weird combination of rotten fish and moldy old cheese.

"Who are *you*?" he says, staring at us strangely.

"I'm Andy," I say, "and this is Terry and that's Jill. Who are you?"

"I'm the captain of the ship that was wrecked in the storm last night."

"Don't worry, we'll look after you," says Jill. "I'll get my flying cats to airlift you and your crew back to the treehouse."

"I'm sorry," says the captain. "I must be delirious . . . I thought you said *flying cats*."

"I did," says Jill. "This is Silky and her twelve flying cat friends."

228

229

One got bucked off
and then there were seven.

Seven unlucky pirates
making a rockin' pirate mix ...

THUMP!

274

275

325

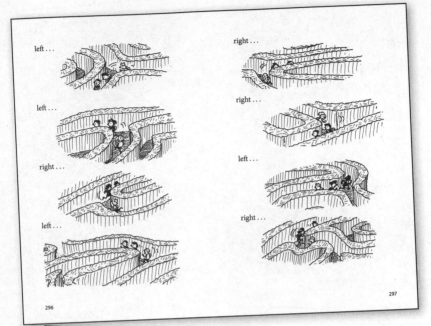

"It's really good," says Jill when she's finished. "I *love* stories with a happy ending."

"Me too!" says Terry.

"But that's the thing," I say. "It's not going to have a happy ending unless we get it to Mr. Big Nose on time."

"Why don't we use Captain Woodenhead's cannon?" says Terry. "We can put the book in it and blast it straight to him. It'll get there in no time!"

"Great idea!" I say. "Let's load it in."

"It's really good," says Jill when she's finished.
"I *love* stories with a happy ending."

"Me too!" says Terry.

"But that's the thing," I say.
"It's not going to have a
happy ending unless
we get it to Mr. Big Nose
on time."

"Why don't we use
Captain Woodenhead's
cannon?" says Terry. "We
can put the book in it and
blast it straight to him.
It'll get there in no time!"

"Great idea!" I say. "Let's load it in."

"Okay," says Terry, "all done. Can I light the fuse?"

"Sure," I say.

I hand him a match.

333

"Hey, that looks like fun!" says Jill. "Can I try it?"
"No problem," says Terry. "Hop in!"

338

"So that's it," says Terry. "We're finished! Do we have free time now?"

"We sure do," I say. "Our next book isn't due for at least a year."

"Great," says Terry, "because I've drawn up a set of plans for another thirteen stories that I'd really like to get your opinion on ..."

Andy Griffiths lives in a 26-story treehouse with his friend Terry and together they make funny books, just like the one you're holding in your hands right now. Andy writes the words and Terry draws the pictures. If you'd like to know more, read this book.

Terry Denton lives in a 26-story treehouse with his friend Andy and together they make funny books, just like the one you're holding in your hands right now. Terry draws the pictures and Andy writes the words. If you'd like to know more, read this book.

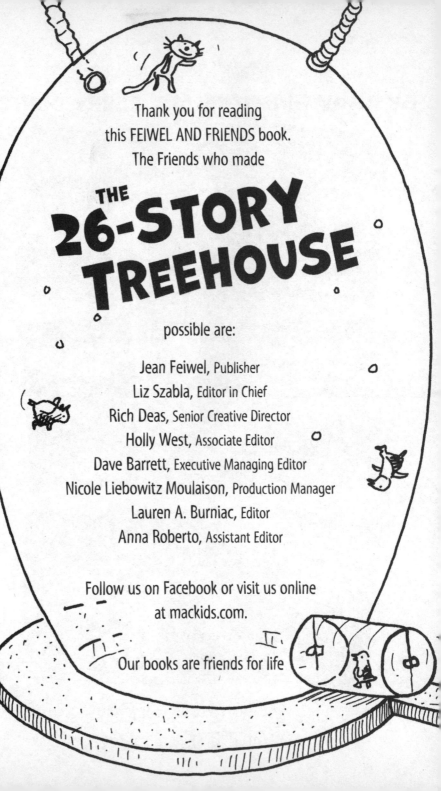

Thank you for reading
this FEIWEL AND FRIENDS book.
The Friends who made

THE 26-STORY TREEHOUSE

possible are:

Jean Feiwel, Publisher

Liz Szabla, Editor in Chief

Rich Deas, Senior Creative Director

Holly West, Associate Editor

Dave Barrett, Executive Managing Editor

Nicole Liebowitz Moulaison, Production Manager

Lauren A. Burniac, Editor

Anna Roberto, Assistant Editor

Follow us on Facebook or visit us online
at mackids.com.

Our books are friends for life